THE ICE CREAM MYSTERY

created by
GERTRUDE CHANDLER WARNER

Illustrated by Hodges Soileau

ALBERT WHITMAN & Company
Morton Grove, Illinois

ISBN 0-8075-5535-5

3 5 7 9 10 8 6 4

Printed in the U.S.A.

The Boxcar Children Mysteries

Contents

CHAPTER 1

A Horse Named Butterscotch

"Benny? Benny, where are you?" called ten-year-old Violet from the back door of the big white house.

No one answered.

"Benny?" Violet called again.

"Haven't you found him yet?" asked her sister, Jessie. "Henry's waiting."

Henry was fourteen and the oldest of the four Alden children. Benny, six, was the youngest.

"He and Watch were playing ball," Violet said. "But I don't see them now."

"I know how to get Benny's attention. Watch this!" said Jessie, taking charge. She was twelve and liked to get things done.

Cupping her hands to her mouth, Jessie shouted, "Benny! Watch! *Ice cream!*"

Almost immediately a small boy and a small dog came running from behind the old boxcar that stood at the edge of the backyard. "Here we are," the boy cried. Watch barked happily.

Violet laughed. "Benny! You're all muddy," she said.

"We are?" Benny looked down at his dirt-streaked T-shirt. Then he looked over at Watch, whose whole face from nose to ears was powdered with sticky dirt. "Oh," he said. "I guess we did get a *little* dirty. I was helping Watch dig a hole to bury a bone."

"I'll wash Watch with the garden hose," Jessie said. "Violet, why don't you help Benny get his hands and face clean."

"Aw, do I have to clean up already?" Benny said.

"If we're going to get ice cream, you do," Violet told him.

"Ice cream? Well, I guess I *could* wash up a little bit," said Benny. He followed Violet into the house.

"And put on a clean T-shirt," Jessie added.

"Awww," said Benny, but he didn't argue. Benny would do almost anything for ice cream.

A little while later, Violet and Benny came hurrying down the front steps of the house. Jessie, Watch, and Henry were waiting.

"There you are," said Henry, jumping to his feet. He picked up his bicycle. "Let's go."

It was a hot day, so Watch rode in Jessie's bicycle basket instead of running beside them. But he was still panting gently by the time they reached the Greenfield Ice Cream Barn at the edge of downtown Greenfield. The small shop was built to look like an old-fashioned red barn. Behind that was a real red barn with a small fenced-in pasture on one side. A neat gray shingled house with red trim stood just down the road. The owner of the shop lived there.

The Aldens steered their bikes into the bicycle stand in front of the store, and Watch hopped out of his basket. But instead of leading the way to the Ice Cream Barn where he knew he would get some water and maybe a taste of vanilla ice cream, he scampered toward the big red barn.

"Watch!" exclaimed Benny. "Where are you going?"

Watch barked.

"Okay, I'm coming," said Benny, as if he could understand what Watch had said.

Henry looked at his sisters and shrugged. "I guess we'd better go see what Watch is up to," he said.

They found Watch in the pasture next to the barn. He was nose-to-nose with a large tan horse with a cream-colored mane and tail. Benny was scratching the horse's ears.

"Look! Watch and I found a horse. A big horse!" said Benny.

"There's never been a horse here before," said Jessie.

"What's your name?" Violet wondered in a soft voice.

"That's Butterscotch," a voice said behind them. "She's a new business partner at the Ice Cream Barn. And so am I."

The Aldens turned to see a tall girl, with bright green eyes and a thick ponytail, coming out of the barn. Her hair matched the color of Butterscotch's coat. She had on jeans and a red shirt with the words ICE CREAM BARN embroidered in gold above the pocket.

"Hi," said Benny. "Who are you?"

"Benny, don't be rude," said Jessie.

The girl laughed. "Don't worry about it," she told them. "I'm Brianna. I've just moved to Greenfield to join the ice-cream business."

"I'm Jessie. This is Violet, Henry, Benny, and Watch," said Jessie.

"How can Butterscotch be in the ice-cream business?" asked Henry.

"Why don't we go get some ice cream and I'll explain," Brianna suggested.

Inside, the shop was white with red trim. Old photographs of farmers and farm scenes decorated the walls. Gingham curtains hung in the windows.

Katy, the owner of the Ice Cream Barn, stood behind the red counter in a long white apron. She had just handed a customer a scoop of vanilla on a sugar cone.

The customer, a blond woman with thick, dark eyebrows and a stiff frown, said, "This is a single scoop?"

"Yes," said Katy. She cocked her head and looked at the enormous mound of vanilla ice cream. The Ice Cream Barn was well known in Greenfield for its big servings. The Aldens knew that the woman couldn't be from Greenfield or she would have known that.

The woman pushed her sunglasses farther back on her head and stared at the scoop of ice cream.

Katy grinned. "If that's not enough, I could add a little more."

"Where?" Benny whispered to Violet. The cone looked very full already.

"It's too much!" the blond woman declared. "How can you stay in business with such big single scoops?"

"It's a mystery!" said Katy cheerfully. "But our customers just keep coming back. Big scoops, exciting flavors, that's our specialty."

The woman sighed, as if Katy had said something upsetting. Then she turned away, balancing the vanilla ice cream carefully, and took a seat at a small table near the window.

Katy looked over at Brianna and the Aldens and winked. She was a small woman with a big pile of black and silver hair wound in a bun on top of her head, almost like a swirled ice-cream cone. Her eyes were chocolate-brown.

"I'll take care of these customers," Brianna said, motioning toward the Aldens.

"Okay, but wash your hands," Katy said. She smiled at Benny, then disappeared through the door to the kitchen.

"Yes, ma'am!" said Brianna, laughing.

Soon Henry was digging into an ice-cream float with chocolate ice cream. Jessie

had chosen peanut chunk swirl with chocolate sprinkles, while Violet had cherry
vanilla in a dish. Benny picked two scoops,
one of pistachio and one of the special flavor of the week, double lemon pie.

"A mix like that might give some people
a stomachache," Brianna said as she handed
Benny his double scoop.

"Not me," said Benny. "Not my cousin
Soo Lee, either. She lives in Silver City and
she likes ice cream, too. But she's on vaca-
tion with Uncle Joe."

"We'll still be serving ice cream when
Soo Lee gets back," Brianna promised as
she set a bowl of water outside the door for
Watch. Next to it, she put a dish with a little taste of vanilla ice cream. Then she
poured herself a glass of water and leaned
on the counter across from the Aldens.

Benny's eyes got round. "Don't you want
ice cream?" he asked Brianna.

"There's such a thing as too much ice
cream, Benny," Brianna said.

Benny looked shocked. "No, there isn't,"
he argued.

Everyone laughed and Benny smiled a little sheepishly.

"It's too bad we can't take some chocolate mint chip back to Mrs. McGregor," said Violet. "She loves the chocolate and the little green mint chips. And the ice cream is extra good today."

"Who is Mrs. McGregor?" asked Brianna.

"She's our housekeeper," Violet answered. "We live with her and our grandfather."

"We used to live in a boxcar in the woods," Benny added. "Just by ourselves. That's where we found Watch. And then Grandfather found us."

"We were orphans and we didn't know we had a grandfather who wanted us," explained Jessie.

They told Brianna all about how they'd found the old boxcar in the woods where they'd lived until their grandfather, James Alden, found them and took them to live with him in his big old white house in Greenfield.

"And now the boxcar is in our backyard," concluded Henry.

"Grandfather put it there for us," Violet explained. "Now we use it as a playhouse."

"That's an amazing story," said Brianna.

Just then Katy bustled back in. "Well," she said, "I'm glad to see my favorite customers and my favorite granddaughter have met."

"I'm your only granddaughter, Granna Katy," Brianna answered, laughing again.

"Granddaughter? But you said you were the new partner," Jessie said.

"That, too," Brianna agreed. "Katy's favorite and only granddaughter, and her new partner."

"You said Butterscotch was a new partner, too," Henry reminded her.

"Does Butterscotch test ice cream for you?" guessed Benny.

"Good grief, no!" Katy exclaimed. "What an idea!"

Brianna said, "What flavor of ice cream did you say Mrs. McGregor likes?"

"Your chocolate mint chip," said Violet.

"What has that got to do with Butter-scotch?"

"It's a surprise. A mystery," said Brianna.

"We're good at solving mysteries," Benny said promptly. "We've solved lots and lots of them."

"I can guarantee you'll have this one solved by this afternoon," said Brianna.

"How?" Violet wanted to know.

"You'll see," said Brianna. No matter how many questions the Aldens asked before they left the ice-cream shop, she wouldn't give them even a single clue to help them solve the mystery.

CHAPTER 2

A Melted Ice Cream Mess

Violet heard it first. She and Benny were sitting on the front porch later that afternoon giving a tea party for her dolls and Benny's stuffed animals. Watch was sleeping in a patch of sunlight nearby.

Ding, ding, dingaling, a bell chimed from not very far away.

Violet looked up. She carefully set down a doll-sized teacup.

Ding, ding, dingalinggggg. The sound was getting closer and louder.

Suddenly Violet jumped to her feet. "Look!" she cried.

Around the corner and down the street came a large, tan-colored horse.

Henry and Jessie looked up from the bicycle they were repairing on the front lawn.

"It's Butterscotch," Benny said excitedly, jumping up so suddenly that his stuffed bear fell facefirst into the plate of imaginary cookies.

"It *is* Butterscotch," said Jessie.

"And she's pulling a wagon," said Henry.

As the wagon got closer, Henry began to laugh. "I know that wagon! That's Sam and Susie's wagon." Sam and his horse Susie had driven an ice-cream wagon in Greenfield every summer for as long as anyone could remember. "Brianna is inside!"

The wagon pulled up in front of the big white house. "Whoa, girl," said Brianna, and Butterscotch stopped and turned her head to look at the Aldens lined up on the sidewalk.

Watch jumped off the porch to trot over and touch noses with Butterscotch.

"Isn't that Sam's wagon?" Henry asked.

"It was," said Brianna. She jumped down and patted Butterscotch's nose. "I bought it from him. He and Susie have retired, you know. But Sam wanted the ice-cream wagon tradition to continue, so he passed it on to me."

"I'm so glad the wagon didn't retire," said Violet.

"So that's how Butterscotch is a partner in the Ice Cream Barn. She pulls the ice-cream wagon just like Susie used to pull it," Jessie said.

"That's right," said Brianna with a smile, as she looped Butterscotch's reins over a fence post.

Climbing back into the wagon, Brianna opened a sliding wooden panel on one side. Then she reached down into a freezer inside the wagon, pulled out a small container, and set it on the counter of the window. "For Mrs. McGregor," she said.

"Chocolate mint chip ice cream, right?" asked Henry.

"Right." Brianna winked at Benny. "If

you hurry and give it to Mrs. McGregor, it won't melt one bit."

"Wow, is Mrs. McGregor going to be surprised," said Benny. He took the container of ice cream and hurried into the house. A moment later he came hurrying out with a carrot in his hand. "This is for Butterscotch," he said a little breathlessly.

"She'll love it," said Brianna.

Violet stroked Butterscotch's velvet nose as the horse nibbled the carrot from the palm of Benny's hand. Jessie and Henry admired the wagon. "New paint," Henry said.

"Ice Cream Barn colors: red and white," explained Brianna.

Just then a man came hurrying up the sidewalk.

"A new customer," Jessie said in a low voice to Brianna.

But she was wrong.

The man, who had crew-cut hair and an unfriendly expression in his blue eyes, stopped and put his hands on his hips. "What's all this?" he demanded.

"The Ice Cream Barn's new ice-cream

wagon. From our barn to your neighborhood," Brianna said proudly.

"Do you have a permit?" the man said, scowling.

"Yes," Brianna answered. "Of course."

"Oh," said the man. He glared at the wagon, then at Butterscotch. "Noise. Bells ringing, children screaming for ice cream," he said. He wrinkled his nose. "And stinky horse smell."

"Butterscotch doesn't smell!" Benny protested.

"That's what you think!" the man said.

Jessie, who had been staring at the man in wonder, suddenly said, "You're our new neighbor, aren't you? You just moved in at the end of the street."

"Nosy, aren't you?" said the man. "Yes, I'm your new neighbor. My name's Bush. Ronald Bush. *Mr.* Bush to you."

"Welcome to the neighborhood, Mr. Bush," said Violet politely.

"Are you trying to be funny?" the man said. Before Violet could answer, he went on. "Let me warn you. If that horse makes a mess, or you make one bit of noise, I'm going to call the police and complain!"

With that, Ronald Bush turned and stomped back up the street.

The Aldens and Brianna stood and watched until he had disappeared into the house at the other end of the block.

Then Benny said, "You know what, I don't like Mr. Bush."

Brianna shook her head. "Some people are just cranky, Benny. Well, I'd better get going. We have a few stops to make today before I head back to the barn."

"Will you be back?" Violet asked.

"Oh, yes," Brianna said. "We have a bell we'll ring to let people know we're here. We'll park right over there by the curb and people can come and buy ice cream."

"Every day?" Benny asked.

"Not every day, Benny. Greenfield's not *that* small. But at least two or three days a week," Brianna promised.

"Even though Mr. Bush doesn't want you to?" asked Violet.

"Hey, it'll take a lot more than Mr. Bush

to stop this ice-cream wagon," Brianna said. She picked up the reins. Then she said, "You know, you don't have to wait for the ice-cream wagon to come to you. Why don't you come visit us. We'll be closed for business tomorrow, but Granna Katy and I are going to be there early working on some new flavor ideas. Stop by and we'll give you a tour."

"That would be great!" said Jessie.

"We'll be there," Henry added.

"See you tomorrow, then," Brianna said. "Giddyup, Butterscotch."

The next morning, Benny was up early, ready to go. "Are you sure you don't want to come with us?" he asked Grandfather.

"Not today, Benny," James Alden told his youngest grandson, his eyes twinkling. "Maybe next time."

"Okay," said Benny. "Then we'd better hurry. We don't want to be late."

"We just finished breakfast, Benny," Violet protested.

"Brianna said she'd be there early," Benny insisted.

"If we ride our bikes the long way into Greenfield, maybe we won't get to the Ice Cream Barn too soon," Henry said.

A few minutes later, the Aldens pedaled down the street. They waved to their neighbor Ms. Dalby, who was standing in her garden. They waved to Violet's classmate Catherine, who was walking down the sidewalk. They even waved to cranky Ronald Bush when they rode by his house. But Mr. Bush didn't wave back. He stared at them as if he couldn't believe his eyes.

When they reached the Ice Cream Barn, the front door was locked.

"Uh-oh," said Benny.

"We'll wait," said Violet.

They sat down on the bench outside the shop. Then Henry said, "It looks as if someone else is waiting for the shop to open." He nodded in the direction of a small white car parked across the street. They could see someone inside, but whoever it was had on a hat. It was hard for the Aldens to see the driver's face.

"Maybe whoever it is doesn't know the Barn is closed today. I'll tell the driver," Jessie said. She jumped up and started toward the white car. But before she could take two steps, the car pulled away.

"Oh," said Jessie, stopping in surprise.

"Maybe the person wasn't waiting for the shop to open. Maybe whoever it was just stopped to read a map," said Violet.

"I guess," said Jessie.

Just then, Brianna drove up. "You're nice and early," Brianna said as she got out of her car.

"Benny thought we should be," Henry said, laughing.

"Yes," said Benny. "We beat you. And Katy!"

Katy, who had just walked up to the shop from her house, smiled. She said, "Well, let's go in the back way, since we're not open today." She led the way around the side of the Ice Cream Barn and stopped so suddenly that Jessie, who was right behind her, almost crashed into her.

"Oh, no," said Katy.

"What?" asked Brianna.

Katy pointed. A small stack of square white boxes and two large containers, all decorated with a blue stripe, stood by the back door. The box labels read MARTINE BLUE RIBBON ICE CREAM VENDORS.

"Those look like ice-cream sandwiches," Katy said. "But . . ."

Brianna rushed past her and pried open the lid of the top box. "They *were* ice-cream sandwiches. Now they're just a melted mess."

"These say 'Vanilla Ice Cream,' " Violet said, leaning over to inspect the printing on the side of the two large containers. "Five gallons each."

"Vanilla ice-cream soup," said Henry, observing the milky puddle spreading out from the bottom of one container.

"Here's a bill taped to the back door," said Brianna. "It's from Marcos. I don't believe it!" She turned to Katy. "Did you order ice cream for today, Granna?"

"Of course not!" Katy said, shocked. "We're always closed on Tuesdays and Marcos knows that. We never take deliveries on Tuesdays."

"Maybe he forgot," said Benny.

"Marcos would never forget something like that," said Katy.

Brianna unlocked the back door and pushed it open. They followed her through a small storage room. On their left were the tall, gleaming doors of a large walk-in freezer. Next to the freezer was a short hall leading to a closed door with the word OFFICE painted on it.

Katy said, "Brianna, why don't you show the Aldens around while I make a few phone calls and try to find out from Marcos what happened."

Brianna nodded. She took a deep breath and smiled a little. "Mistakes happen," she said. "It's just too bad this had to happen just as we're trying to expand our business."

"It'll be okay," Violet said sympathetically.

Brianna smiled again. "Thanks, Violet. Okay, folks, here's where the grand tour of the Ice Cream Barn starts. We're standing in the main storage room. On the shelves over here are the supplies we use most often: straws and napkins and sprinkles and nuts. Those shelves hold our dishes for sundaes, our glasses for ice-cream floats, and so forth. That big stainless steel door opens onto our walk-in freezer."

"Wow, that's a lot of ice cream," Benny said, peering inside.

"It's actually pretty small for a walk-in freezer," Brianna said. "I've seen much bigger ones. But unlike some places, we don't keep our ice cream for a long time. Granna thinks it changes the flavor, and I agree."

"What do you do with ice cream you don't sell, then?" asked Henry.

"Throw it away. But that hardly ever happens," Brianna said. "We know just how much to make and how much to order. Granna Katy has been in this business for a long time. Anyway, over there is our big refrigerator, for supplies that don't need to be in the freezer, like whipped cream."

Brianna led the way into a small room with high windows. In the middle was a stainless steel object that looked sort of like a very old washing machine. "And this is where we make our own ice cream."

"Wow," said Henry.

"Amazing," said Jessie.

"It works more or less like a small ice-cream maker," Brianna explained. "We put in cream and eggs and sugar and flavorings, and the ice-cream maker churns the ingredients and freezes them to the right texture and temperature. But it takes longer and makes lots more ice cream than the kind of machine you can buy for your home."

"Is that what you use to make new flavors of ice cream?" Violet asked.

"Not right away. First we use a regular ice-cream maker to make very small batches of the flavors. If we like them, then we use this machine to make bigger batches and try them out in the store."

They went back out into the storage room and Brianna reached up and took down two smaller ice-cream makers from a shelf.

They'd just set them on the counter when Katy joined them. She was frowning.

"Did you reach Marcos?" Brianna asked.

Katy looked up and her frown deepened. "I did," she said. "But he says he didn't make a mistake. He says that someone called and placed an order with him and told him to leave it out back first thing this morning."

"Who?" demanded Brianna.

"I don't know," said Katy. "He remembered the order, because he had trouble hearing it. He thought it was a bad phone connection. He wasn't sure if the caller was male or female. Whoever it was, the person said he or she worked for us. The caller claimed to be the new assistant we hired because we were going to be open seven days a week."

"So it wasn't a mistake," said Jessie.

Katy said, "No, Jessie, it was not a mistake. Someone did it deliberately. But why?"

CHAPTER 3

Hard Work and Free Ice Cream

There was a long silence.

Then Brianna said, "Maybe it's somebody's dumb idea of a funny joke."

"Not funny," snapped Katy. "Expensive. We're going to have to pay for that ice cream even though we can't sell it. With all the costs of buying the ice-cream wagon, the new equipment for it, and Butterscotch, we're really going to have to watch every penny now."

"What if it's not a joke?" asked Jessie

slowly. "What if someone did it to hurt you?"

"If it's not a joke, then, well, I don't know what to think," said Katy. "Who would want to do this to us?"

Brianna seemed to hesitate for a moment. Then she shook her head firmly. "No one would," she said. "No one would want to hurt our business."

Henry asked, "Who knows you order from Marcos's company?"

"Anybody who has seen his truck parked outside and him unloading it," Katy said.

"Or anyone who has seen the signs in here," Brianna said, pointing. "We label all the ice cream we order from Marcos and we label our own special flavors and treats so customers will know which is which."

"Oh," said Henry.

"That's not much of a clue, then," said Violet.

"Well, I've told Marcos to only take de-livery orders from me from now on," Katy said. "And he's going to call before he delivers, just to make sure."

"That's good," said Brianna.

"Making ice cream would be good, too," Benny hinted.

Katy smiled at him. "You're right, Benny. Let's get started. Any ideas about new flavors?"

"Peanut butter," said Benny.

"Chocolate anything," said Henry.

"Maybe both," suggested Jessie.

"And crunchy, too," added Violet.

"Sounds delicious! Let's gather some ingredients, then," said Brianna. Violet was relieved to see her smiling again.

Later that day, as the Aldens wheeled their bicycles home, their stomachs too full to ride, they talked about the prank at the Ice Cream Barn.

"I just don't believe it was meant to be a joke," said Jessie. "It was too mean."

"I agree," said Henry. "But why? And who? It could be anybody."

"I think Brianna has an idea about someone who could have done it," said Violet softly.

"I noticed that, too," said Jessie. "When Katy wondered who might do something like that, Brianna almost said something. But then she stopped."

"Do you think whoever it is will play any more jokes?" asked Benny.

"I don't know, Benny," said Henry. "But I do think we should keep a sharp eye out for clues — and for more trouble."

"I think you're right," said Jessie. "I think it's the beginning of a mystery."

"I know," said Benny. "I could get a job at the Ice Cream Barn and look for clues that way!"

"I don't think you're quite old enough yet, Benny," said Violet.

"Are you sure?" said Benny.

"But it's not a bad idea, Benny," said Henry. "Maybe I'll see if they want to hire me. I'm old enough. I'll go back tomorrow and talk to Katy and Brianna."

* * *

The next day, Jessie, Violet, Benny, and Watch waited on a bench in the park near the ice-cream shop while Henry went to talk to Katy and Brianna about a job. Benny was very excited. If Henry got a job at the Ice Cream Barn, he would be able to watch for suspects. *And maybe*, Benny thought, *he'd be able to bring home lots of ice cream!*

So when Henry came walking toward them a little while later, Benny bounced up, shouting, "Did you get the job? Did you?"

Henry grinned, but he shook his head. "No. But I did get some interesting information."

He sat down on the bench and began to pet Watch.

"What did you find out?" Jessie asked.

"Well, they can't afford to hire anybody right now, for one thing," Henry said.

"We should have guessed," said Violet.

"I offered to help out until they could afford to pay me, but Katy said no," Henry went on. "She said they already had to let one assistant go and he would be the first one they hired back when they could."

"Katy fired someone?" asked Jessie.

"Yes. When Brianna came, she laid off an assistant named Preston. Brianna's doing his job and driving the ice-cream wagon," said Henry. "To save money."

"That must have made Preston very unhappy," Violet said softly.

"Yes," agreed Jessie. "Maybe unhappy enough to call in a phony order."

"How do we prove it?" Benny asked. "We have to find clues."

"One way we can do that is by checking out the Ice Cream Barn and its customers," said Henry.

"We can't just show up and stay and stay and stay," objected Jessie. "That would look very suspicious. And weird."

"No, we can't do that," said Henry with a smile. "But even though they couldn't hire me as an assistant, I did get a job. For all of us."

Benny's eyes widened. "What?" he asked. "Driving Butterscotch?"

"No, nothing that exciting, Benny. But Brianna's having a bunch of fliers and posters printed up. We're going to help deliver the fliers and put the posters up all around Greenfield this afternoon. In return, we get gift certificates for free ice cream. Five scoops each!"

That afternoon, the Boxcar Children loaded up their backpacks and bicycle baskets with fliers and posters and tape. Violet and Henry went in one direction. Benny and Jessie and Watch went in another direction.

They put fliers on front stoops and in stacks on the counters of stores. They asked for store owners' permission, and soon posters advertising the Ice Cream Barn and the new ice-cream wagon, pulled by "The Amazing Butterscotch," hung in the windows of the hardware store, the pet supply shop, the bicycle shop, and just about every other store in town.

Jessie and Benny even put up a poster on the bulletin board outside the mayor's office at Town Hall. They'd just hung a poster on a telephone pole near the post office when they met Mr. Bush.

He scowled harder than ever when he saw them.

"Hello, Mr. Bush," said Jessie politely.

"Hi," said Benny.

Mr. Bush leaned over to peer at the poster. "Take it down," he said.

"What?" asked Jessie, startled.

"Take the poster down, or I will," said Mr. Bush.

"Why?" asked Benny.

"Because you're defacing public property," Mr. Bush said. "You can't put posters up without permission. Do you have the permission of the phone company to use their telephone pole for advertising?"

"Uh, no," admitted Jessie.

Watch barked once. Mr. Bush didn't notice. Benny squatted and put his arm around the dog. "Shhh," he warned.

"Then take the poster down," Mr. Bush said. He folded his arms.

Jessie didn't know what else to do. She

took the sign down. As she rolled it carefully, Mr. Bush snorted. 'The Amazing Butterscotch,' indeed," he said in a scornful voice. Then he went into the post office without another word.

"He's really, really mean," said Benny.

"I guess he's right, though," said Jessie.

Benny wasn't listening. "Really mean. Mean enough to play that melted-ice-cream joke," he said.

Jessie blinked. "I hadn't thought about that, Benny," she said. "I guess he could have."

"I think he did," said Benny.

"We'll have to talk it over with Henry and Violet. Let's put up the rest of the posters and then find them."

"Okay," said Benny. To Watch he said, "Come on, boy. And if you see Mr. Bush, you can bark as much as you want!"

They found Henry and Violet outside the bookstore, talking to a tall, lanky boy not much older than Henry. The boy had straight black hair and round black glasses.

He was pointing at the poster in the win-

.dow as Jessie, Benny, and Watch came up to them.

"So you're the ones who've put up the posters all over Greenfield," he said.

"Yes," said Jessie. "The Ice Cream Barn is expanding."

"And they hired you to put the posters up," the boy went on.

"I guess you could say they did," Henry began.

The boy narrowed his eyes angrily. "They hired you — two of you! — and they fired *me*. Said they couldn't afford me!"

"Well, they're not exactly paying us — " Jessie started to explain.

But the boy didn't let her finish. "Fine," he said. "Just fine. But they're going to be sorry they didn't keep me around. You'll see." He turned and almost ran away, his cheeks red with rage.

"Good grief!" said Jessie. "I think we just met Preston."

"He's mad, too," said Benny.

Violet said, "He's mad, *too*? What do you mean, Benny?"

"Mr. Bush got mad at us for putting up posters just now," Benny explained. "By the post office."

"Oh," said Violet.

"Benny thinks Mr. Bush might be the one who phoned in the fake ice-cream order," Jessie explained. "And after the way he acted just now, I think Benny could be right."

"Maybe," said Henry. "Or it might be Preston. He seems pretty upset."

"I wonder if Brianna suspected Preston," Jessie said.

"I don't know," Henry said. "But now we've got *two* suspects."

"And a mystery," said Benny.

CHAPTER 4

Who Took the Posters?

"No dessert?" Grandfather Alden sounded surprised. "Not even you, Benny?" The Aldens had just finished dinner together. Grandfather knew that Benny *always* had room for dessert.

"I had ice cream this afternoon," Benny said. "Two free scoops."

"Big ones," said Henry. "We all had ice cream this afternoon — although none of us had quite as much as Benny did."

"I thought none of you seemed very hungry," said Grandfather, a twinkle in his eye.

"We got paid in ice cream," Violet explained. "For delivering fliers and putting up posters."

"You told me about putting up the posters, but not about the ice-cream payment," Grandfather said.

"We didn't think you'd think it was such a good idea to eat ice cream so close to dinner," explained Benny.

"Noooo, I don't. But I guess you won't do it again," Grandfather said.

"No," said Violet. "Not even to solve the mystery."

Grandfather nodded. His four grandchildren had told him all about what had happened at the Ice Cream Barn. He knew if anybody could find out who had placed the fake order, it was them.

"Will you be going to the Ice Cream Barn tomorrow?" he asked.

"Probably," said Henry. "Then we can look for more clues."

"But I don't think we're going to eat as much ice cream," said Jessie. "Even Benny has had enough for a while!"

* * *

But the Aldens didn't go to the Ice Cream Barn the next morning. Instead they did a few errands for Grandfather and Mrs. McGregor. They mailed letters for Grandfather. They took Mrs. McGregor's books back to the library. Then they stopped by the bike shop to put air in Benny's bicycle tires.

That was when Violet noticed that the poster she had put up in the front of the bike shop wasn't there.

She stopped. She looked at Henry. "Didn't we put a poster up right over there, yesterday afternoon?" she asked.

Benny looked, too. "Yes," he said. "Where is it?"

"It isn't there," said Jessie.

"Maybe the owner of the store took it down," said Henry.

"But he said we could put it up," Violet reminded him.

They went inside. As soon as he saw them, Louis, one of the store's owners, smiled and said, "More posters today?"

"No. I mean, yes, maybe," said Jessie. "Because the poster we put up yesterday isn't there. Did you take it down?"

"No," said Louis in surprise. He called over his shoulder to a woman repairing a bicycle. "Thelma, did you take that ice-cream shop poster down?"

"Nope," Thelma answered.

"Okay, thanks," said Jessie. They turned to go. Then Jessie turned back. "If we bring another poster, may we put it up in the window?" she asked. "On the inside?"

"Sure," said Louis. "No problem."

But there was a problem, the Aldens soon realized. Most of the posters they'd put up the day before had been taken down. Only the shops where they'd put posters on the insides of the windows still had posters up. And many of the places where they'd left stacks of fliers had no fliers left, either.

None of the store owners knew what had happened to the posters or the fliers. No one had seen them disappear.

"Maybe different people picked up all the fliers one at a time," said Violet doubtfully.

"I don't think so," said Henry. "We put out too many fliers to be taken in one day. I think whoever took all the posters got rid of all the fliers they could find, too."

"Someone who doesn't like the ice-cream shop," Benny said.

Jessie nodded in agreement. "And we need to find out who."

"But now we'd better put up more posters," Violet said. She added, "And put out more fliers."

"Good idea. Let's go," said Henry. "And while we're at the Ice Cream Barn, I think we need to talk to Brianna."

"Why?" asked Benny.

"Because she knows something she's not telling us. It might be a clue," said Henry.

"Back for more ice cream today?" Katy called cheerfully as the Aldens came through the front door of the shop. She was serving a double scoop to one of two boys, while a familiar-looking thin blonde woman in sunglasses was poking at an ice-cream sundae in the corner. As Jessie glanced over, the woman slid a small notebook out from under her napkin and wrote something on it before hiding it under her napkin again.

"Not yet," said Henry. "We thought we'd put up a few more posters and hand out some more fliers."

"Great," said Katy. "We have another big boxful out in the barn. Brianna's out there. She can show you."

The Aldens found Brianna outside the barn. She had a paintbrush in her hand and was studying something she had set on a small table covered with newspaper. Butterscotch watched sleepily from the shade of a nearby tree.

"What's that?" asked Benny, skipping up to the table.

"Oh, hi. This? It's a suggestion box. I just painted it. When it's dry, I'm going to put it inside the shop. Customers can write down their ideas and opinions and stick them inside," Brianna explained.

Violet bent forward to study the small wooden box. "It looks like the ice-cream wagon!" she said.

"It does? Good. It's supposed to," Brianna said. "What's happening?"

"Well," said Jessie. "We have a problem."

"Someone took all our posters!" blurted Benny.

"And most of the fliers, too," added Violet.

"What?" Brianna said, her voice going up.

"We came to get more to put up," said Henry. "And we need to ask you a few questions."

"Good grief," said Brianna. She paused, thinking hard, then asked, "What questions?"

"There are at least two people we know about who don't like the Ice Cream Barn. One is our neighbor, Mr. Bush," Jessie said.

Brianna nodded.

"The other is Preston, Katy's old assistant," Henry said.

"Why would Preston hate the Ice Cream Barn?" Brianna said, looking very surprised. "He loved working with Granna Katy."

"We met him yesterday when we were

putting up fliers," Violet said. "He was very upset about losing his job."

"But it is only temporary, until we can pay him again!" Brianna protested. "You don't think — do you think Preston made that fake order? And stole the posters?"

"Maybe," said Violet.

"No! No, that's not possible. I know Preston is upset, but he'd never do something like that," said Brianna. "And Mr. Bush is just worried about having the wagon in the neighborhood. When he sees how well behaved Butterscotch is, he'll get over it."

"If Preston and Mr. Bush didn't do it, who did?" asked Henry.

"At first I wondered if another ice-cream company might be trying to put the Ice Cream Barn out of business. National Sugar Shop Corporation has been asking Granna Katy to sell them the Ice Cream Barn so they can set up their own ice-cream shop in Greenfield," said Brianna. "But then I realized that was silly. A big company wouldn't bother trying to hurt a small business like ours."

"Anyone else?" asked Jessie. She looked toward the Ice Cream Barn. A white truck with a bright blue stripe all the way around it had pulled up to the front of the shop. The door of the truck read, MARTINE BLUE RIBBON ICE CREAM VENDOR AND RESTAURANT SUPPLY COMPANY. "How big is Marcos' company? Could he be the one trying to hurt the Ice Cream Barn?"

"Martine Supply is not very big. Marcos is one of three partners there," Brianna said. "But he'd never, ever try to harm the Barn's business. We're old customers of his. Katy's known him for years." She nodded toward the truck. "In fact, I have a meeting with Marcos and Katy in about five minutes."

"We need to get the fliers," Henry reminded her.

"Oh, right. In the stall next to Butterscotch's in a big box on a bench. You can't miss them." Brianna carefully picked up the almost dry suggestion box. "Well, I'd better get to that meeting."

As soon as she'd left, the Aldens loaded

up with fliers and posters. Then Jessie said, "Come on. Let's go meet Marcos!"

Inside, the store was quiet. The ice-cream sundae the blonde woman had been eating was melting on the small table by the front window. Katy and Brianna were sitting at a larger table with a stocky man with black and silver hair who had thick horn-rimmed glasses. He was wearing a white shirt with a blue stripe that matched the truck outside.

"Hi," said Jessie. "We found the posters and fliers, Katy."

"Good," said Katy. "The more you put up, the better it is for business."

"Would you like one?" Benny asked, handing a flier to the man.

"What's this?" the man said, examining the flier.

"Advertising," Brianna replied.

"And this is your advertising staff?" the man said, grinning.

Brianna grinned back, then introduced everyone. "As you know, we buy our basic flavors — vanilla, chocolate, strawberry — from Marcos," she explained to the Aldens.

"He also provides some of our ice-cream treats, such as ice-cream sandwiches."

"If your business grows like you want it to, you're going to need more than basic flavors from me," Marcos said. "You'll never have time to make all the special flavors you do now."

"Someone was just saying that to me a few days ago," Katy commented. "She had lots of ideas to make us into a big business. If we hired her to run things, she said, we'd be ice-cream kings."

"Good thing she didn't convince you," Brianna said. "We don't want to be ice-cream kings, or queens, or anything like that. We just want to make the best ice cream around."

"You do!" said Benny.

"I have to admit, it tastes very, very good. But you could give your flavor recipes to my company and we could make batches for you, you know," Marcos said.

"No," said Katy firmly. "And I'm not going to change my mind, no matter what you say."

Holding up his hands, Marcos said, "Okay, okay. Maybe you're not going to change your mind . . . yet."

"Make a note and put it in our new suggestion box," Brianna said with a wink.

Marcos laughed. "See you next week," he said, and got up.

"Don't forget our order forms," Brianna said, handing him several sheets of paper.

Marcos tucked the papers into a folder. "If you want to change your order, you know where to reach me," he said. He waved and headed out the door.

"The suggestion box looks good," Violet said admiringly.

"It does, doesn't it?" Katy said in a pleased voice. "I hired the right business manager and partner when I hired my granddaughter."

Brianna blushed, but she looked pleased, too.

"I have a suggestion," Henry said briskly. "I suggest we get to work putting up these posters and handing out these fliers."

"Tell you what," Brianna said. "When you're finished, stop back by here and I'll give you a ride on the ice-cream wagon."

"Hooray!" said Benny.

"We'll be back," Jessie promised.

CHAPTER 5

Is This Your Horse?

"Next stop, the library," Brianna announced from the driver's seat of the ice-cream wagon. She guided Butterscotch across the grass and under the shade of a large old oak tree next to the library building. "Why don't you ring the wagon bell, Benny."

Benny leaned forward and gave the bell a long, loud ring. "I'm getting good at this," he announced.

"You sure are," Brianna agreed.

The Aldens had been riding in the ice-cream wagon all afternoon, taking turns sitting up on the driver's seat with Brianna, helping dish up ice cream, peering out the top half of the Dutch door at the back of the wagon.

Now, as the wagon halted, Henry unlatched the Dutch door, pushed it open, and walked around to Butterscotch. He took the reins from Brianna and tied Butterscotch to the tree.

Jessie helped lower the steps from the driver's seat, while Violet pushed open the side window from which the ice cream was served.

Brianna went to join Violet inside the wagon, but Benny stayed up in the wagon seat. He liked being there. He waved at everybody he saw and called out, "Ice cream sold here!"

Now he talked excitedly. "Look! There's Thelma from the bike shop! Hi, Thelma. I've seen lots of people I know today. Marcos, in his blue and white truck. I like his truck. It's not as nice as our wagon, though.

And I saw three neighbors from our street. And two friends of Grandfather's."

Listening to Benny chatter, Jessie patted Butterscotch's nose, then filled her water bucket. Brianna always carried a container of water in the wagon just for Butterscotch.

"Ice cream! Sold here!" Benny sang out from the wagon seat. "Hi, come buy some ice cream! Oh, hi, Preston."

Preston didn't ask how Benny knew his name. He stopped his bike a few feet away. "So now you're all working for the Ice Cream Barn."

"No," said Jessie. "Brianna's just letting us ride in the wagon today."

"Ha," said Preston. But he didn't sound angry. He sounded almost as if his feelings were hurt.

"It's true," said Henry.

"Sure," said Preston.

On the other side of the wagon, a small line was forming at the window. Brianna was very busy scooping ice-cream cones

while Violet took the money and made change.

"How's Butterscotch?" asked Preston abruptly.

"Fine," said Henry.

"Come pet him," urged Jessie.

"Hot day, cold ice cream!" Benny called from the seat to some passersby. Jessie had thought of that and he liked the sound of it.

Butterscotch snorted, making bubbles in the water, then raised her dripping nose to look at Preston.

He got on his bike and pedaled away without another word.

Brianna and Violet hadn't noticed Preston. They were too busy. The small line of customers had gotten bigger.

"The special flavor this week? Banana split," Brianna said. "Is that what you want, Ralph?" By now, she knew many of the regular customers by name. "One scoop coming right up."

A large group of children came out of the library and joined the line. Brianna greeted several of them by name, too.

"How do you remember everybody?" asked Violet.

Brianna grinned. "Lots of them ask for the same thing every time. That makes it easier. Like Annie with the red hair is one scoop chocolate, one scoop vanilla, vanilla on top. Maria is chocolate cherry fudge. Radj, the boy at the end of the line? He'll order one scoop of whatever the special is, with sprinkles. He always gets sprinkles, no matter what flavor the ice cream is."

"May I pet the horsie?" a little girl asked.

Henry said, "Her name is Butterscotch and she likes to have her nose petted. You can scratch behind her ear, too."

Butterscotch was almost as popular as ice cream with the group of children. One little boy even tried to share his ice cream with the big horse. Jessie stopped him in time, explaining that Butterscotch would have plenty of oats when she got home from work that night.

Benny didn't say anything about that. He thought it was too bad that Butterscotch couldn't have an ice-cream cone of her own.

Then Violet reached down to hand a customer change and looked up to find herself almost face-to-face with a police officer.

"Oh!" she said. "Hello. Would you like some ice cream?"

"No, thank you," said the police officer. "I'm Officer Pierre. Who's in charge here?"

"I am," said Brianna.

"Could I see your license and permits?" the police officer asked.

"Sure," said Brianna. She washed her hands, then opened a small drawer underneath the money drawer. She took out a folder and passed it through the window to Officer Pierre.

The officer examined the papers carefully, then handed them back to Brianna.

"Is there a problem, Officer?" Henry asked.

"We have the library's permission to park the wagon here," Jessie added.

Officer Pierre didn't answer right away. She walked around to look at Butterscotch, who was standing quietly, her eyes half closed. Officer Pierre glanced at the water bucket, then back at the wagon. "Hot day," she said.

"Hot day, cold ice cream," said Benny promptly.

That made Officer Pierre smile a little.

The officer moved closer to Butterscotch, stroking her nose and looking her over carefully. Then she said, "We had a complaint about the horse. Someone said she was being mistreated."

"Butterscotch? Mistreated?" gasped Brianna in disbelief.

"She's not being mistreated!" Henry said. "We always stop in the shade. And she gets water at every stop."

"And she has her own barn and stall and paddock," said Jessie.

"And oats at night," Benny said.

"Who complained?" Violet asked.

"I'm not allowed to say," Officer Pierre replied. "But whoever said you were treating your horse badly obviously didn't know what they were talking about."

"Or whoever it was wanted to cause trouble," Henry said in a low voice.

Neither Officer Pierre nor Brianna heard him, but Jessie did. She glanced over quickly and Henry knew she'd been thinking the same thing.

"Butterscotch and I don't go out during the hot part of the day. And if it is too hot — or too cold — we won't go out at all," Brianna was saying.

"I'm writing this complaint up as unfounded," Officer Pierre reassured her. "That means there is nothing to it, and if we get another complaint, we'll look much more closely at it before contacting you."

"Good," said Benny.

After the officer had left, Brianna and Violet served a few more ice-cream cones to customers, including one more familiar face. It was the blond woman with the dark eyebrows. "One scoop," Brianna predicted in a low voice as they watched the customer approach. "And no matter what flavor, she won't eat it all."

Brianna was right.

"What's your freshest ice cream?" demanded the woman.

"It's all fresh," Brianna told her.

"The ice cream you *just* made," the woman said.

"Our special flavor, banana split," said Brianna.

"I'll take it. One scoop," the woman said.

She looked the wagon over as she waited for her scoop.

"Would you like to pet Butterscotch?" Jessie asked.

"The horse? No, thank you," said the woman. She paid for her cone and took a careful taste. "It *is* fresh," she said.

"Yes, it is," said Violet.

The customer walked around the back of the wagon, still looking it over. Then she left, taking tiny, careful tastes of her ice cream.

Benny saw her toss it into a trash can across the street.

"She threw it away!" he said in horror.

"Do I know my customers, or what?" said Brianna. "She does that every time."

They had a few more customers, but it was getting late now. When the last one had left, Henry unhitched Butterscotch from the tree, emptied the water bucket, and tied it to the side of the wagon. He and Jessie climbed in the back while Brianna joined Benny on the driver's seat. Violet closed the Dutch door and latched it, and then went to the front of the wagon to peer through the little window behind the driver. "Ready," she said.

"Giddyap, Butterscotch," Benny said.

"Home, girl," said Brianna, and Butterscotch, who knew that was where they were going anyway, turned in the direction of the Ice Cream Barn — and her own barn, too.

Inside the wagon, Jessie said in a low voice so Brianna wouldn't hear her, "I think whoever complained about Butterscotch was trying to cause more trouble for the Ice Cream Barn."

"I think so, too," said Henry. "Anyone can see that Butterscotch isn't being mistreated."

"It was a mean thing to do," said Violet. "It upset Brianna. But who could have done it?"

"Remember Benny saying he'd seen Marcos? It could have been Marcos. Benny waved at him, so Marcos knew the ice-cream wagon was making its rounds," said Jessie.

"So did Preston," said Jessie. "And he was just here, right before the police officer came."

"He sure was," said Henry. "He was here *and* he was in a very bad mood. And he asked about Butterscotch."

They looked at one another. Violet said, "It doesn't really prove anything. And the one who complained about Butterscotch before was Mr. Bush."

Henry frowned. "True." He paused, then said, "Wait a minute." Going to the front of the wagon, he spoke through the window. "Benny, remember you said you saw some of our neighbors today?"

"Yes," said Benny. "I waved at them."

"Was Mr. Bush one of them?" asked Henry.

"Yes," said Benny. "He was still cranky. He didn't wave back. I think he's the one who made the police come after Butter-scotch."

Henry suddenly laughed. "Could be, Benny. But we can't prove it."

He went back to join Jessie and Violet. "You heard what Benny said," Henry told them. "We have to count Mr. Bush as a suspect, too."

Violet sighed. "This isn't good," she said. "We still have three suspects. We still don't know who's trying to sabotage the Ice Cream Barn. I wish we could find out, before anything else happens."

Sometimes wishes come true. But this time, Violet's wish didn't.

CHAPTER 6

Nasty Notes and Sticky Clues

Katy met them at the door of the shop. In each hand, she held several slips of paper. "Can you believe this? Some people!" she fumed, waving the papers in the air.

"What is it, Granna?" asked Brianna, jumping quickly down from the wagon and tying Butterscotch to the front step rail.

"Someone stuffed the suggestion box full of blank slips of paper," said Katy. "I noticed all our suggestion slips were gone —

and the pencil, if you can believe that — so I opened the box and found this."

She stormed back inside, followed by Brianna and the Aldens. The top of the suggestion box was open. Dozens of suggestion slips had been crammed inside.

"They're not all blank," said Henry. "This one says, 'Caramel is my favorite flavor. Make ice cream with caramel in it.'"

"And this one says, 'Can you make bubble gum ice cream?'" Brianna read.

"Ick," said Violet.

"I don't know," said Jessie. "It doesn't sound so bad."

Katy made a face. "It takes all kinds," she said.

"Here's another. It says . . ." Violet's voice trailed off.

Brianna read over her shoulder. "'You're a terrible ice-cream shop. Why don't you close and give someone who knows how to make ice cream a chance?'"

"Oh, that's terrible," said Benny.

"And this one says, 'Greenfield doesn't need a new, improved Ice Cream Barn. No matter how much you improve, you'll still be no good. Give up now.' "

"That's not true!" said Brianna furiously. "And we're not giving up."

"Do you recognize the handwriting?" Henry asked Brianna and Katy.

"If I did, do you think I'd just be standing here?" Katy said. "Besides, the writer has obviously tried to disguise it. Look at those big block letters."

Just then the phone rang. Katy picked it up. "Ice Cream Barn," she said. She didn't sound as cheerful as she usually did. She listened and frowned. "No . . . No! . . . The answer will always be no. I already told you. I — we — don't want to be a big business!"

When Katy hung up, she turned to Brianna. "That Jean Johnston keeps calling. I wish she would stop! Her ideas are good, but she just won't listen when I tell her we don't want to make the Ice Cream Barn into that kind of business."

Brianna made a face.

"Did you notice anyone hanging around the suggestion box?" asked Jessie, getting back to the business of finding clues. "Marcos? Preston? Someone else?"

"Marcos? He was in earlier to try out the new flavor, just as he usually does. But he didn't go near the suggestion box. And I haven't seen Preston for a while." Katy looked puzzled. "But it's been so busy today. The ice-cream wagon has brought in a lot of new customers lately. When it was busy I hardly looked up, and when it was quiet I went to the back to work on new flavor ideas. I just came out whenever I heard the bell ring or saw a customer who needed ice cream."

Brianna shook her head in disgust. "Disguised handwriting. Nasty notes. Crank calls about Butterscotch . . . Okay, I'm beginning to be convinced that this is more than someone's idea of a joke."

"Preston, Marcos, Mr. Bush," said Jessie as the Aldens sat on the porch that night after dinner. Grandfather rocked quietly in the swing, with Benny yawning and leaning against him.

"Mr. Bush," murmured Benny sleepily.

"He's a good suspect," said Jessie. "He's been around every time something has happened. He knew we'd put up the posters. He'd already complained about Butterscotch even before someone called the police today. He could have stuffed the suggestion box without Katy noticing."

"Preston, too," said Violet.

"Didn't you tell me Katy said she hadn't seen Preston?" Grandfather asked.

"Yes, but maybe he sneaked in when it was really busy. In disguise," argued Violet.

"He *could* have," Henry said doubtfully. "But don't you think Katy would have recognized him?"

"A hat, dark glasses, a fake mustache," Violet began, then suddenly giggled. "Wow, Preston would look pretty silly, wouldn't he?"

"It would be the kind of disguise everyone would notice," added Henry. "And Katy and Brianna still seem to trust Preston."

"So we move Preston to the bottom of

our list of suspects," said Jessie. "That still leaves Marcos."

"Yes," agreed Violet. "But I still feel like we're missing a very important clue. I'd like to go to the shop tomorrow morning to ask Katy a few more questions."

But the Aldens were in for a shock when they reached the Ice Cream Barn early the next day. A big sign was stuck to the front door. CLOSED, the sign read. OUT OF BUSINESS.

"What?" gasped Violet.

"There are more signs over here. They're all over the place!" Benny cried.

Sure enough, almost the entire front of the Ice Cream Barn had been plastered with CLOSED and OUT OF BUSINESS signs.

"I don't understand," Henry said.

Katy and Brianna drove up and parked the car. Katy got out, holding a grocery bag. She stopped. Her mouth dropped open in astonishment.

"Is it true?" Benny asked. "Are you closed?"

At the same time, Katy said, "What's this? Who did this to the Ice Cream Barn?"

They were all silent for several long moments. Katy and Brianna stared speechlessly at their shop. The Aldens looked from the shop to Katy and Brianna, and then back again.

Finally Henry said, "You didn't do this?"

"No!" said Katy. She shut the car door, hard. "I sure didn't."

"I don't believe this," Brianna said. Her lips tightened. "It's going to take forever to get all those signs down. Those aren't just taped up. They look glued."

"No, it won't," Benny said. "We'll help."

Brianna smiled a little at this. "Thanks, Benny."

"We'd better get started," said Jessie. "Leaving those signs up is bad for business."

They all worked hard, and as fast as they could. But it still took them all morning to get the sticky signs off the door and windows. After they got the signs down, they scraped off the glue. Finally, they washed and polished all the glass.

"This is what I *don't* want to be when I grow up," Benny said. "A window washer!"

"It's hard work," agreed Violet.

A navy blue car pulled to the curb. A short man in a pinstripe suit got out stiffly. He looked at the Aldens and Brianna and Katy and at the buckets and towels and rags. He looked at the freshly cleaned windows. "Nice windows," he said. "Where could I find the proprietor of this shop?"

"If you mean you want to talk to the boss, that's me," Katy said. "Who are you?"

"Gerald Smithers, National Sugar Shop Corporation," the man said, extending a hand.

Katy dried her hand and shook his. "I've already told someone from your company that I'm not interested in selling this place."

"So I understand," Mr. Smithers said smoothly. "I came to see if you've reconsidered."

"You're wasting your time," said Katy. "I said I won't sell my business and I'm not going to."

Mr. Smithers fished in his pocket and

brought out a business card. He held it out and Henry, who was closest, took it. "If you change your mind . . . *when* you change your mind . . . give me a call," Mr. Smithers said. He smiled at them all, got in his car, and drove away.

"You want this card?" Henry asked Katy. Katy shook her head.

"Well," Brianna said as the car disappeared from sight. "We've got clean windows and an empty suggestion box. Who's ready for ice cream?"

"It's been two days, and I've still got glue stuck to me from all those signs in the windows of the Ice Cream Barn," Jessie complained. She was sitting on the stump that served as a step up into the old red boxcar in the backyard.

"It makes it easy to catch the Frisbee," Benny said. He, Henry, Violet, and Watch were playing Frisbee.

"It's been quiet at the Ice Cream Barn the last couple days," Henry noted. "Maybe whoever was playing all those nasty tricks has decided to give up after all."

"Maybe," said Jessie thoughtfully. "Or maybe they're planning something really big."

Henry caught the Frisbee and held it. He stared at his sister. "What do think might happen?" he asked.

"I don't know," said Jessie. "But ever since I saw that man from the National Sugar Shop, I've felt, I don't know, funny. He seemed so confident that Katy would give up and sell the Ice Cream Barn to him."

"Should he be a suspect, too?" Violet asked.

"He wasn't around when any of those things happened," Jessie said. "At least, none of us saw him. But I wouldn't mind asking him a few questions."

"We can do that," said Henry.

"How?" asked Benny.

"We can call him. He gave us his business card, remember?" Henry said. "I still have it — Katy said she would never need it."

He'd barely finished speaking when Jessie leaped to her feet. "Let's call," she said, and led the way to the phone. Henry dialed the number on the card, then handed Jessie the phone. She waited impatiently while it rang.

"Hello, Mr. Smithers?" Jessie said. "My name is Jessie Alden and I — "

She didn't get to finish. Mr. Smithers said, "If you're calling about the jobs at our new shop, we're conducting interviews this afternoon."

"Jobs?" said Jessie.

"At our new shop in Silver City," said Mr. Smithers. "Corner of Main and Nugget. Can you find it?"

"Yes," said Jessie. "Thank you." She hung up the phone.

"That was quick," commented Henry.

Jessie looked at the others. "Well," she said, "I guess we'd better get to Silver City this afternoon."

"Why?" asked Benny.

"To see Mr. Smithers about a job," said Jessie.

CHAPTER 7

The Sugar Shop

Fresh paint glistened on the shop at the corner of Main and Nugget in nearby Silver City. Hanging in the front window was a sign that read, NOW HIRING. HELP WANTED FOR THE SUGAR SHOP OF SILVER CITY.

"There's Mr. Smithers's car," Jessie said, pointing to the big dark car parked next to a small white one in the parking lot.

"And there's Mr. Smithers," said Benny. "He's talking to one of our customers!"

"What?" Violet said.

They all looked through the window. Mr. Smithers was sitting on a folding chair next to a big packing crate. A blond woman with dark eyebrows was sitting on another folding chair next to him. Papers were spread out on the packing crate and she was talking rapidly while Mr. Smithers nodded.

After a while, she stood up, gesturing for Mr. Smithers to keep the papers. Then she shook hands with him and came hurrying out the door. She'd just reached the white car when she saw the Aldens.

"Hi," said Benny.

"Oh!" she said. "Uh, hi, there."

"Are you going to get a job at the Sugar Shop?" asked Jessie.

"A job? How . . . uh, maybe," said the woman. She flung her briefcase in the car before jumping in herself and quickly driving away.

"She seems kind of nervous," said Violet.

"If she just had a job interview, maybe she is," said Jessie. "Come on, let's go talk to Mr. Smithers."

Mr. Smithers glanced up from the papers when the Aldens walked in. Jessie said, "Mr. Smithers, I called you this morning — "

"Oh, no, no," he said. "You're too young for a job with us. You have to be at least fourteen."

"I'm fourteen," said Henry. "But — "

"Here, fill out this application," said Mr. Smithers, snatching up a piece of paper from the packing crate.

"But I don't want a job, thank you," said Henry, handing the application back.

That got Mr. Smithers's attention. "What do you want, then?" he said. "I'm a very busy man. I have to hire counter help, managers . . . and who knows where I'm going to find a good manager, someone with experience. I've seen people with interesting ideas" — he tapped one finger on the papers — "but not enough experience. Well? Well?"

"How long have you known you were opening a Sugar Shop in Silver City?" asked Jessie.

"A few months now," said Mr. Smithers.

"Then why did you try to buy the Ice Cream Barn?" asked Benny.

"It's a good business. Buy the shop, buy the customers. When that didn't work, we thought about putting a shop in Greenfield. But we decided that the Ice Cream Barn customers were, er, too loyal. So we settled on Silver City," explained Mr. Smithers.

A phone began ringing in the back of the half-finished shop.

"If you'll excuse me," he said. He jumped up and was gone.

"Thank you," Violet said to his back.

Outside on the sidewalk, Jessie said, "A Sugar Shop in Silver City. I wonder if Brianna and Katy know about it."

"If they don't, we should tell them," Benny said.

"Do you think Mr. Smithers is a suspect?" Henry asked.

"No," said Jessie. "I did for a minute, but I don't think someone who works for a big company like that would do such petty dishonest things to a small business like the Ice Cream Barn."

"I don't know about that," said Henry.

"I wonder if Preston knows about the Sugar Shop," said Violet. "He has experience. He could get a job there."

"If we see him, we'll tell him," said Jessie.

But they forgot about telling Preston anything when they reached the Ice Cream Barn. A big sign on the door of the shop said, CLOSED.

"Oh, no," groaned Henry. "Not again."

But Benny was peering through the glass. He tapped on the window. "Katy is inside," he explained.

A moment later, Katy opened the door. "Come in, come in," she said urgently, her expression grave. "Did you see Brianna? Have you found Butterscotch?"

"Found Butterscotch? What are you talking about?" Violet said in shock.

"You don't know, then? Butterscotch is missing. Brianna went into the barn this morning to let her out of her stall into the paddock and she was gone," said Katy.

"Gone! How did she get out?" asked Jessie.

"Someone took her, that's how." Katy sank down into a chair. "There's no way Butterscotch could have gotten her stall door open and the barn door as well. And I don't think she would have closed those doors behind her, either."

"Someone *stole* Butterscotch?" Benny cried. "A horse thief?"

"A horse thief," said Katy. "Poor Butterscotch. I wonder if we'll ever see her again."

"Don't worry, you will," said Jessie stoutly. "We'll find her."

"I wish you could," said Katy hopelessly. "I wish you could."

"Let's go to the barn. We can start looking for clues there," said Violet. She patted Katy's hand. "It will be all right," she promised.

"No lock on either the barn door or the paddock door," said Henry. "But no way

Butterscotch could have gotten either of those open herself, even if she did get out of her stall."

"The ice-cream wagon is still here," noted Jessie.

"It would be hard to hide an ice-cream wagon," said Benny. "But I guess you could, if you can hide a boxcar." Benny was remembering the time their boxcar had gotten stolen.

"No footprints we can use," said Violet, bending over to examine the hard-packed earth outside the barn door. "Just scuffs in the dirt."

"Whoever took her either had to lead her away, ride her away, or drive her away in a horse van," said Henry. "If they drove her, they could be anywhere."

"And anybody," said Violet in a discouraged voice.

"No!" said Jessie. "Not just anybody. I think whoever took Butterscotch is the same person who phoned in that fake delivery order, who stole the posters, who complained about Butterscotch, and who made those horrible suggestions."

"And put up the 'Out of Business' signs," added Benny.

"Preston — " began Jessie.

As if Jessie had made him appear by saying his name, Preston came running toward the barn. He stopped, looking wildly around. "She's gone," he said. "She's really gone."

"Yes, Butterscotch is missing," said Henry.

Preston's face was pale. He looked as if he might be about to cry. "Who would do a rotten thing like that?" he said.

"Someone who wanted to put the Ice Cream Barn out of business," said Henry. They all watched Preston closely.

Preston didn't seem to notice. "That's one of the reasons I was so upset when Katy laid me off," he said, almost to himself. "I wanted to help with Butterscotch. I thought it would be cool to learn about horses and how to drive the wagon. Poor Katy. She must be really upset."

Preston straightened his shoulders. "Katy said you were looking for Butterscotch. I will, too. And if I can do anything else to help, let me know."

"We will," said Violet.

Preston turned and walked slowly back to the store.

The Aldens stared after him. Then Violet said, "He *could* be pretending to be upset so we wouldn't suspect him."

"He could, but he'd have to be an awfully good actor," said Jessie.

"Preston didn't steal Butterscotch or do any of those other things?" asked Benny.

"I don't think so, Benny. He seems to really care about Katy and Butterscotch and the Ice Cream Barn. I think Katy is right to trust him," Henry told his little brother.

"Okay. That leaves Marcos and Mr. Bush," said Violet. "One of them is a horse thief."

"It's Mr. Bush," Benny said triumphantly. "I told you so. Let's go arrest him and get Butterscotch back!"

CHAPTER 8

Who Did It?

"Hold on, Benny. Just because you think Mr. Bush did it doesn't mean we can go arrest him. We have to have proof," Violet said.

"If we got Butterscotch, wouldn't that be proof?" asked Benny.

"It would. But I don't think Mr. Bush is keeping Butterscotch in his backyard. It would be very hard to hide a horse in our neighborhood, at least for very long."

"So he has Butterscotch at a farm or a

stable," said Benny. "Maybe he owns a farm," he added.

"Maybe." Jessie thought hard for a moment. "There is only one stable nearby, just outside Silver City."

"But there are lots of farms," said Violet, feeling discouraged.

"If Butterscotch is at a farm — or the stables — she'd have to get there in a truck or van," Jessie said. "It's too far to ride her or lead her."

"Marcos has a van for deliveries," Violet said.

"Maybe Mr. Bush has a van or truck, too," said Henry. "We need to check that out."

"And we need to check on the stables, to see if Butterscotch is there," said Benny.

"Let's see when Katy expects Marcos again," suggested Violet.

Nodding, Jessie said, "And after that, let's make a few phone calls."

Henry hung up the pay phone. "Nope, no new horses at the Silver City Stables," he reported.

"I didn't think there would be," Jessie said. "It would be one of the first places the police would look, just like we did."

"Let's go get Mr. Bush," Benny urged.

"Let's go *talk* to Mr. Bush, you mean," said Violet.

"Okay. Let's go," said Benny. He tugged on Violet's sleeve.

"Not right now," Henry said. "We have to get home. It's almost time for dinner."

"We'll talk to Mr. Bush first thing tomorrow," Jessie told Benny.

The Aldens rode their bicycles slowly home. They were tired and sad. Benny kept remembering how awful he had felt once when Watch had disappeared.

Watch came bounding up to greet them when they got home. That made them all feel a little better as they wheeled their bikes into the garage.

Then, suddenly, Watch ran toward the street. He ran up to a bicyclist who was pedaling by on the sidewalk. He barked.

"Watch, no!" said Benny, hurrying after him.

The bicyclist stopped. Watch stopped.

"Sit, Watch!" Jessie called. Watch sat.

"You know you're not supposed to chase bicycles," Benny scolded. Then he looked up at the bicyclist. "Oh!" he said in surprise.

The others had reached the sidewalk by then and had seen who the bicyclist was, too.

"Hello, Mr. Bush," said Violet politely.

"Uh-oh," Jessie said very softly to Henry. She was sure Mr. Bush was going to be very angry about Watch barking at him.

But Mr. Bush surprised them all. "Well," he said to Watch. "At least you're a dog who knows how to mind his manners when he is told."

"Watch is very smart," Benny said.

Mr. Bush looked up. "Smart enough," he said. He bent and gave Watch one quick pat on the head.

"Do you like to ride bicycles?" Jessie asked.

"I wouldn't be riding one if I didn't," Mr. Bush said. "I think it makes more sense than driving. Besides, I don't have a driver's license. Don't want one. If I can't get some-place by bike, a bus is good enough for me." He stopped, as if he was surprised at how much he'd said.

"I like riding in the ice-cream wagon," Jessie said boldly. "A horse is a good way to travel, too."

Mr. Bush gave Jessie a sharp look. Then he said, "Well, a horse might be better than a car. But I don't like horses. Never have. One stepped on my foot when I was ten years old. Broke two toes." He winced as if he could still feel the broken toes.

"I'm sorry," said Violet.

"What for? It was a long time ago," said Mr. Bush. With that, he got on his bicycle and pedaled away.

The Aldens stood for a moment in amazed silence.

"Mr. Bush didn't do it," Benny said at last.

"I guess not," said Violet. "It doesn't sound like he'd get close enough to Butter-scotch to steal her. And if he did, he wouldn't be able to drive her away."

"That leaves Marcos, then." Henry looked at his wristwatch. "We should go back to the Ice Cream Barn tomorrow at lunchtime. Katy said he'd be by then for next week's orders."

"I can't believe it's Marcos," said Violet. "I hope it isn't."

"If it's not," said Benny, "then who is it?"

The next day, Marcos was just getting out of his familiar white truck with the blue stripe when the Aldens pedaled up to the front of the Ice Cream Barn.

"Let's help him unload," whispered Jessie. "Then we can check out the back of the truck and look for clues. Maybe there will be pieces of hay or a few horse hairs inside."

They hurried over to meet Marcos just as he swung open the double back doors of the truck. They stopped and stared.

The truck was lined with shelves. There was no room for a horse the size of Butterscotch. Not only that, but it was refrigerated and very cold.

"Hey, there," said Marcos. "Cold enough for you?" He laughed heartily at his bad joke. Then he said, "It's a traveling freezer, you see? No melted ice cream for me."

Jessie couldn't give up. "Have you talked to Katy yet?" she asked. "Or Brianna?"

"No. What's wrong?" Marcos suddenly looked worried. "Is Brianna okay?"

"They're both fine," said Violet. "It's Butterscotch."

Marcos looked puzzled.

"The horse who pulls the ice-cream wagon," Benny said. "She's been stolen!"

"Stolen! When? What happened?" Marcos said.

"Someone took her out of the barn last night," Violet told him. "We don't know who."

"That's terrible," said Marcos. "Just terrible!" Shaking his head he took a small box out of the back of the truck and closed the doors. "Samples of new ice-cream products," he explained. "I thought Katy and Brianna might like to try them before they place their next order. Maybe it will cheer them up a little, too. I know how they liked that horse."

The Aldens walked with him into the store. Brianna was at the ice-cream counter serving customers.

She smiled when she saw them, but it wasn't much of a smile. "I'll get Katy," she told Marcos.

A moment later, Katy came into the store.

"I heard about your horse," said Marcos. "I'm sorry. I'm sure you will find her."

"I'm sure we will, too," said Katy, but she didn't sound sure.

Marcos handed her the small box of frozen treats. "New treats from my company for you to try," he said.

"Thank you," said Katy. She looked down at the box as if she didn't know what to do with it.

"Thanks, Marcos," Brianna said. "Give it to me, Granna. I'll put it in the freezer behind the counter for now."

Katy handed the box over, then sat down at one of the tables.

"How is business?" Marcos asked.

"Business is good," Brianna said, then turned to wait on a family that had come in for ice cream.

"I'm glad to hear it," said Marcos. "Because I have an idea for the Ice Cream Barn. I was describing your ice cream to a friend who is the chef of a small restaurant and he is very interested in it."

"Interested?" repeated Katy.

"Yes. He'd like to order some of your special flavors for his dessert menu. I told him you were a small company and I didn't know how much extra you could make, but I think you could handle this."

"Sure we could," said Brianna, who somehow could serve the customers and listen to Marcos and Katy at the same time. "If I'm not going to be driving the ice-cream wagon . . ." She paused, then went on, "I could make the extra batches of ice cream."

"Or when you get your horse back, you could hire extra help," Marcos said.

"Yes," said Brianna. But she sounded no

more convinced than Katy about Butterscotch's return.

Benny had wandered over to stare at the ice cream in the freezer, but Violet, Henry, and Jessie had settled at a table near Katy and Marcos. Now they looked at one another. Marcos didn't sound like a man who had stolen a horse — or one who wanted the Ice Cream Barn to go out of business.

"I like that idea, Marcos," said Katy. "It's nice of you to think of us."

Marcos grinned. "You'd need to order more supplies from me to make the extra ice cream," he added. "So it would be good for *my* business, too. And, of course, I'd want to be the one who delivers the ice cream to the restaurant."

Brianna grinned.

"It would take some planning," said Katy. She paused. "Let me give you our order for next week, then we'll talk this over more."

The shop bell jingled as a customer walked in.

Katy looked up for a second and frowned slightly.

"May I help you?" Brianna asked.

"It's her," Violet said in her quiet voice.

"Who?" asked Benny. He looked, then said, "Oh! She's the customer who never eats her ice cream."

"I'd like to try your Haystack Sundae," the woman said, reading from the menu board behind the counter.

"Coming right up," said Brianna.

"Mmm," said Benny as the customer walked out of the shop a few minutes later with a scoop of butter pecan ice cream drizzled with caramel and smothered with slivered almonds.

Benny kept watching as the woman stopped at the curb to taste the sundae. She slid into her car and took another bite and then another. Then she rolled down her window and dumped the rest of the sundae into the trash can.

Benny gasped. "Look," he said to Violet. "She threw away her Haystack!"

Jessie and Henry looked, too. As the woman's white car pulled away from the curb, Jessie leaned forward to get an even better look.

Then she ran toward the door.

"Jessie, where are you going?" Henry asked.

Jessie didn't slow down. "Come on, grab your bikes," she said. "We have to follow that car!"

CHAPTER 9

A Clue and a Trap

The four Aldens followed the white car through Greenfield. They stayed as far behind it as they could while still keeping it in sight. The driver didn't seem to notice that her car was being followed.

At last the car turned into a driveway on Walnut Street in a neighborhood on the other side of Greenfield.

"Oh, good," Benny panted. "I was getting *tired.*"

Jessie braked to a stop on the sidewalk a short distance from the house.

"What are we doing? Why are we following that customer?" Henry asked.

Jessie nodded toward the house. "That white car looked familiar," she explained. "Remember that time when we got to the Ice Cream Barn early and a white car was outside? The one that drove away so fast?"

"That's the same car?" Benny asked.

"I think so," said Jessie.

"What is the name on the mailbox?" Benny asked. "I can't read it."

Violet read the name aloud softly.

They all stared at the mailbox. Henry let out his breath. "We've heard that name before," he said.

"Johnston . . . Isn't that the name of the person who keeps calling the Ice Cream Barn?"

Jessie nodded. "The one who wants Katy to hire her to make the Ice Cream Barn a big business."

"Is Butterscotch here?" Benny asked.

"There's no place to hide a horse here," Henry said. "She must be keeping Butterscotch someplace else."

"Then how will we find her?" demanded Benny.

Jessie's eyes had begun to dance. "I think I know how," she said. "I think what we need to do is deliver a fake order."

"A fake order? Of ice cream?" asked Benny.

"No, not ice cream, Benny. Oats," said Jessie.

The Aldens biked home as fast as they could go. They ran into the house and went straight to the phone in the kitchen.

Violet took out the phone book and found the number they needed. "Ready?" she asked.

"Ready," said the others.

Violet crossed her fingers, then dialed the number. She handed the phone to Henry.

"Hello, I'm calling to confirm a delivery for Jean Johnston," Henry said, speaking into the receiver.

"What?" the woman who had answered replied.

"Forty pounds of oats," Henry said. "To be delivered to 53 Walnut Street."

"No. Not for me! Bring it to the Three-Mile Farm. That's where all these deliveries are supposed to go," the woman said.

"That's not the address I was given," Henry said.

"I'm the one who pays the bills, not the one who eats the oats," she said impatiently. "You've got it all mixed up. Take it to Three-Mile Farm. Honestly! What am I going to do with forty pounds of oats? I'll be there tomorrow to meet the delivery."

And with that, Jean Johnston slammed down the phone.

Henry placed the receiver back in its cradle, then turned to his siblings and smiled.

"Three-Mile Farm," said Henry. "I think we've found Butterscotch."

"Let's go get her," Benny urged.

"Not tonight, Benny. We'll go get her tomorrow — and we'll also get the thief," Henry promised. "Now let's call Brianna."

* * *

The big old barn at Three-Mile Farm was very quiet in the middle of the day. But in the field nearby, Mack, the owner, drove his tractor next to the rows of potato plants. Chickens scratched in the barnyard. A sleek cat sunned on a bale of hay, purring loudly.

"It's a good thing we didn't bring Watch," Benny whispered. "He might have wanted to chase the cat."

Benny was crouched next to Violet behind a bale of hay. Across the barn, Henry was hiding behind a stall door. Jessie and Brianna stood near the front of the barn behind some sacks of feed.

"Here comes the car," Jessie called softly. They all crouched down a little lower and listened as a car pulled up to the front of the barn.

Benny wrinkled his nose. "I need to sneeze," he whispered.

"Don't sneeze," Violet told him.

Benny pinched his nose to keep from sneezing.

A car door slammed.

Footsteps pounded through the front of the barn, then halted.

"Hello?" Jean Johnston called.

Everyone held their breath — everyone except Butterscotch, who was standing in her stall, chewing on a wisp of hay.

Jean Johnston walked down the short row of stalls until she reached Butterscotch. "Well," she said crossly. "Why am I here? I'm paying good money for someone to take care of you, and it's his job to meet the feed truck, not mine. You are turning out to be more trouble than it's worth."

Jessie stepped out into the barn behind Jean Johnston, followed by Violet, Henry, Benny, and Brianna. "The only trouble with Butterscotch," Jessie said in a loud voice, "is that you stole her."

Jean Johnston spun around. Her blond hair seemed to almost stand on end. Her black eyebrows shot up.

"No!" she said. Then she saw Brianna and her face grew pale. "Oh, no!" she moaned. "What are you doing here?"

Brianna folded her arms. "Catching a thief who tried very hard to help put the Ice Cream Barn out of business."

"You don't understand," said Jean Johnston. "I just wanted to help you!"

CHAPTER 10

The Mystery Ice Cream

Brianna's eyes widened in amazement. "Help us? You call fake deliveries and 'Out of Business' signs helping us, Jean?"

"Don't forget the suggestion box and the stolen posters," said Jessie.

"And the stolen horse," said Violet. She had gone over to Butterscotch. The big horse had heard voices and put her head over the stall door. Now she lowered it to let Violet scratch her silky ears.

Jean Johnston looked around as if she

wanted to escape. But there was no way out. She took a step back, then sank down onto a bale of hay.

"Why don't you tell us about it," said Brianna in a more gentle tone of voice.

Jean looked up. "I wanted to be the manager of the Ice Cream Barn. I knew I could make it great. With a few changes and the right approach, you could have become a big chain."

"Like the Sugar Shop?" asked Jessie.

"Yes. But Katy kept saying no. I had to do something to make her change her mind," Jean went on. She looked at Brianna. "I thought if Katy started losing money, she would see that she needs me to help run things."

"Is that when you started playing tricks on the Ice Cream Barn?" asked Violet.

"Yes," admitted Jean. "But it wasn't working. Then I heard the National Sugar Shop Corporation was interested in getting into the ice-cream business in Greenfield. I thought if I took Butterscotch, I could upset business enough so that Katy would want to sell the Ice Cream Barn. Then maybe the National Sugar Shop Corporation would hire me," Jean said.

"You kept coming to the shop and eating ice cream," said Benny.

"Sampling the new flavors, taking notes," said Jean.

"Spying," said Henry.

"Companies do that all the time. It's how business works," said Jean.

"Not at the Ice Cream Barn," said Brianna.

"We saw you meeting with Mr. Smithers at the new Sugar Shop in Silver City," said Jessie.

Brianna said, "To apply for the manager's job there."

"Yes. From that job, I could move up in the corporation — especially if I could put the Ice Cream Barn out of business," Jean explained. "That's when I thought up the plan to hide Butterscotch for a little while — right after the interview."

"You know, you didn't have to do all these awful things," Brianna said. "Your business plan and your ideas were very good. I'm sure the Sugar Shop would have hired you just because of that."

"I didn't think good ideas were enough," said Jean bitterly. "Sometimes you've got to be ruthless to get ahead."

"I'm sorry," said Brianna, "but I don't think your terrible behavior got you anywhere."

Then Jean said, "What are you going to do now? Are you going to call the police?"

Brianna shook her head slowly. "No. Not this time. But I am going to call Mr. Smithers to tell him what you did."

"What you did was wrong," said Violet.

"I know," Jean said softly. She wouldn't meet their eyes.

"Don't come back to the Ice Cream Barn," said Brianna.

Jean stood up. "All right," she said, and walked slowly out of the barn. At the door, she stopped and turned. "I'm sorry," she said.

"If you're really sorry," said Violet, "you'll never do anything like this again."

Without answering, Jean went out to her car. A minute later they heard it drive away.

Brianna let out a long breath. "Well," she said. "That's that."

Shortly after that, the farmer came into the barn. "Well," he said, "do you and the horse need a ride?"

Brianna smiled broadly. "Yes, thank you. Butterscotch is going home."

The Aldens were sprawled in the grass in the shade outside their big old white house. Playing soccer had made them hot and tired. Watch had rolled over on his back with all four feet in the air and was panting in his sleep.

Suddenly Benny sat up. "Did you hear that?" he said.

"What?"

Watch woke up and rolled to his feet. He gave a quick bark.

"That!" said Benny, jumping to his feet, too. "The ice-cream wagon."

"It is!" said Violet.

"Oh, good," said Jessie. "I could use some ice cream right now."

"Me, too!" said Henry.

Butterscotch and the ice-cream wagon came into sight and all four Aldens waved enthusiastically.

Brianna waved back and guided the wagon into the driveway.

"Look who is with her! It's Preston!" said Jessie.

Preston jumped down from the driver's seat to tie up Butterscotch. He grabbed the bucket from the side of the wagon.

"You can fill it up from the hose over at the side of the house," offered Henry.

"Thanks," said Preston with a big grin.

"Who wants ice cream?" asked Brianna, flinging the window of the wagon open.

"I do!" said Benny, hopping up and down. He wasn't hot and tired any longer.

Preston came back and set the bucket down. "I heard you were the ones who found Butterscotch," he said admiringly. "That was great! How did you figure it out?"

"Jessie did, mostly," said Violet.

"No, we all did," said Jessie. "We'd eliminated all our suspects and I'd just about given up. Then I remembered a clue and it all came together."

"The thief kept buying ice cream and not eating it," said Benny disapprovingly.

"But we set a trap and caught her," Violet said.

"Found your horse, did you?" called a familiar voice.

Everyone looked up to see Mr. Bush standing on the sidewalk.

"We did," said Brianna.

"So you're detectives," said Mr. Bush.

"We are," said Jessie.

"Hmmm," said Mr. Bush.

"Would you like some ice cream?" asked Brianna.

"Maybe I would," said Mr. Bush.

"You would?" Benny's eyes got round.

"I said I don't like horses, not that I don't like ice cream," said Mr. Bush. He almost smiled. He walked around the wagon, staying well away from Butterscotch, and went

up to the window. "I'd like a sundae, with raspberry ice cream and hot fudge, whipped cream, no nuts, and extra cherries," he said.

"Wow," said Violet softly.

"Good ice cream," said Mr. Bush, after he'd tasted his sundae. Then, still giving Butterscotch plenty of room, he walked on.

"Double wow," said Jessie.

"Who else wants ice cream?" asked Brianna.

"All of us," said Henry.

"Good, because I've got just the flavor for you. And it's on the house. Or the wagon," said Brianna.

She made four enormous ice-cream cones.

Each of them took a taste.

"Butterscotch," said Violet.

"And fudge," said Henry.

"And salted nuts," said Benny.

"Cashews, right?" guessed Jessie. "And something else, too, but I don't know what. It's awfully good, though."

"Mmm. What is it?" asked Violet.

"Our newest flavor," said Brianna. "Mystery Ice Cream for the Ice Cream Mystery."

"It's great," said Henry.

"What do you think, Benny?" asked Brianna.

Benny grinned. "I think that when I grow up I'm going to be a detective — and drive an ice-cream wagon!"

GERTRUDE CHANDLER WARNER discovered when she was teaching that many readers who like an exciting story could find no books that were both easy and fun to read. She decided to try to meet this need, and her first book, *The Boxcar Children*, quickly proved she had succeeded.

Miss Warner drew on her own experiences to write the mystery. As a child she spent hours watching trains go by on the tracks opposite her family home. She often dreamed about what it would be like to set up housekeeping in a caboose or freight car — the situation the Alden children find themselves in.

When Miss Warner received requests for more adventures involving Henry, Jessie, Violet, and Benny Alden, she began additional stories. In each, she chose a special setting and introduced unusual or eccentric characters who liked the unpredictable.

While the mystery element is central to each of Miss Warner's books, she never thought of them as strictly juvenile mysteries. She liked to stress the Aldens' independence and resourcefulness and their solid New England devotion to using up and making do. The Aldens go about most of their adventures with as little adult supervision as possible — something else that delights young readers.

Miss Warner lived in Putnam, Connecticut, until her death in 1979. During her lifetime, she received hundreds of letters from girls and boys telling her how much they liked her books.